COOL STUFF ABOUT ANIMALS

BOOK ONE

**Fun & Facts
For All Those Who Enjoy Learning**

C. Warren Gruenig and Hank Richter

COOL STUFF ABOUT ANIMALS
BOOK ONE
©Copyright 2016 C. Warren Gruenig / Hank Richter

Printed by CreateSpace, An Amazon.com Company

ISBN: 9781545391754

©Copyright renewed 2017

OTHER BOOKS BY THE AUTHORS

COOL STUFF ABOUT ANIMALS
BOOK TWO
©Copyright 2016 C. Warren Gruenig / Hank Richter

Printed by CreateSpace, An Amazon.com Company
ISBN: 9781545392348

©Copyright renewed 2017 C. Warren Gruenig / Hank Richter

A THOUGHT FROM THE AUTHORS

This book is dedicated to all those parents, grandparents
and loving family who encourage children's curiosity
and share together the fun of reading
and the joy of learning, no matter what the age.

DEDICATION

A great debt of gratitude
to our wives, Dee and Janet,
for their considerable help
and support with our book.

ACKNOWLEDGEMENT

This fun project is the result of an idea C. W. had many years ago.
Meeting Hank, who loved to draw, was the start of a perfect collaboration—
C.W.'s research and text and Hank's original drawings to bring it all to life.
Special appreciation to Janet Richter who brought the text and drawings
together into the book you see today.

*Our sincere appreciation to all our many editors—young and old—
for your smiling reviews and thoughtful feedback!*

Let's get started....

Are
Elephants
afraid of
Mice?

They love playing with
everybody!

Can a Kangaroo

be taught

to box?

Yes

Never accept a dare
   to box with one!

Are Owls really the wisest birds?

NO

Owls are not as wise as crows or ravens!

Do Camels
store water
in their humps?

No

Water is stored in their blood
and other body parts,
not in their humps.

Fun Fact: Camels can drink as much as 30 gallons
of water at one time.

Do male Seahorses have babies?

Mommy Seahorses deposit eggs
in the Daddy's pouch.
He carries them until they are born.

Do Sea Otters
wash their hands
before eating?

YES

Sea Otters even wash themselves
all over!

Is it true old Dogs
cannot learn
new tricks?

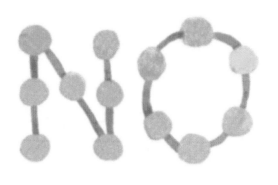

Dogs of any age
can learn new tricks.

Can an Ostrich run faster
than a horse?

Sometimes they can,
but the horse usually wins!

Fun Fact: Ostriches can also roar like a lion!

Do BULLS
charge
the color red?

NO

Bulls charge the movement
of the Matador's cape.
He stands **VERY** still, only waving the cape.

Are Crocodiles slow on land?

NO

Crocodiles can probably
run faster than you can!

Do Guinea Pigs oink
when they eat?

NO

Guinea Pigs only cough, squeak and purr.

Fun Fact: Guinea Pigs are related to Porcupines
and Hamsters. They are not pigs.

Do PRAIRIE DOGS bark at the moon?

NO

Prairie Dogs mostly grunt and whistle.
They only bark like dogs to warn of danger.

Fun Fact: Prairie Dogs are not dogs,
but are related to squirrels and chipmonks.

Are Crocodile tears real?

YES

Crocodiles appear to cry when eating.
When they chew, it squeezes water
out of their eyes!

Are there

GIANT Rabbits?

Yes

One Rabbit in England named Darius
stood 4 feet 8 inches tall
and weighed 49 lbs.!

That's one **BIG** bunny!

Can a Housefly hum on key?

...and always in the key of F!

Do Elephants never forget?

With big brains, Elephants never forget a face.

Fun Fact: Older Elephants even huddle together when they remember how they escaped past dangers.

Are Hen's teeth scarce?

NO

Scientists have found chickens sometimes grow small teeth; however, 80 million years ago when dinosaurs roamed the earth, all chickens and birds had teeth.

Are male Lions lazy?

YES!

Though they roar the loudest,
male lions are lazy.
Mommy lionesses do most
of the hunting.

Are bats blind?

Some see poorly and some see very well. None are blind.

Do dogs see things only in black and white?

They also see dark to light blue
and dark to light yellow.

**You are invited to turn the page
to see two make-you-smile excerpts from**

**COOL STUFF ABOUT ANIMALS
Book Two**

Do Toads give warts?

NO

This myth maybe came when mothers
didn't want children to bring
Toads in the house!

Do Ostriches
bury their heads in the sand
when they are afraid?

Ostriches do listen for danger
with their ear to the ground.

Fun Fact:
Ostriches sometimes
eat sand to help digest
their food.

And now...Meet the Authors

INTRODUCING....

Author C. Warren (C.W.) Gruenig spent thirty-four years serving as an elementary school teacher, master teacher and building principal. Earlier, he and his wife lived in South America surrounded by fascinating animals of all kinds. As a teacher, he became familiar with children's humor and their desire to know facts that other kids, and even adults, don't know. That makes this book perfect for adults and children to share together. It is especially appropriate for parents and grandparents to actively read with children, seeing who might know the answers to the stimulating questions, playfully disagreeing, and then turning the page to find what is true. C. W. takes special pleasure in writing encouraging messages to every child in each book with his signature. This is done with book purchases from the website CoolStuffAboutAnimals.com. C. W. is having fun reading to elementary school children in his local area and is available to speak to clubs and organizations about the humorous surprises about animals.

Hank Richter, illustrator and co-author of "Cool Stuff..." , was born in Cleveland, Ohio. After serving in the military, he attended the renowned Philadelphia Museum School of Art where he excelled in graphic art and was awarded both the Faculty and Alumni scholarships. After graduating with honors, Hank worked for several major advertising agencies as art director before returning to Cleveland where he met and married Bev Loomis. Together they decided to move West to Phoenix where exciting things were happening. Through a challenge from a client, Hank created his first fine art sculpture of an Indian head...and the rest is history! Though primarily a Western artist, his interest in writing and illustrating children's books began when his three daughters were small. Today Hank has produced several themed books with learning challenges and positive moral messages. Along the way, Hank was awarded the Gold Medal for Art Director for "November 11, 1963 – A Child's Eyes", a film about President Kennedy's assassination.

"Cool Stuff About Animals" Book One and Book Two are available on Amazon.com or on www.coolstuffaboutanimals.com or www.artofthecowboy.com.

Made in the USA
Las Vegas, NV
10 May 2021